Disney · PIXAR

5

Minute
Treasury

Bath · New York · Cologne · Melbourne · Delhi
Hong Kong · Shenzhen · Singapore

This edition published by Parragon Books Ltd in 2016

Parragon Books Ltd
Chartist House
15–17 Trim Street
Bath BA1 1HA, UK
www.parragon.com

Mike's Laughing Matter written by Wendy Loggia.
Illustrated by the Disney Storybook Artists.

Radiator Springs Road Trip adapted by Hannah Buchsbaum
from the story *Pit Crew to the Rescue!* written by Chuck Wilson.
Illustrated by the Disney Storybook Artists.

A Super Family adapted by Annie Auerbach from the book *The Incredible Dash*
written by Dennis "Rocket" Shealy and originally published by Random House.
Illustrated by the Disney Storybook Artists.

A New Mission adapted by Annie Auerbach from the story written by Jason Katz.
Illustrated by Alan Batson and the Disney Storybook Artists.

The Ghost-Light Fish written by Laura Driscoll.
Originally published in *Friendship Stories* by Disney Press.

Mixed Signals adapted by Hannah Buchsbaum from the story *Buzz Off* written by Lisa Papdemetriou.
Illustrated by Frederico Mancuso, Giorgio Vallorani and the Disney Storybook Artists.

A Friend in Need adapted by Hannah Buchsbaum from the book *Fish Are Friends, Not Food*
written by Annie Auerbach and originally published by Scholastic, Inc.
Illustrated by the Disney Storybook Artists.

Rematch! adapted by Hannah Buchsbaum from the story written by Susan Amerikaner.
Illustrated by Scott Tilley, Andrew Phillipson, Janelle Bell-Martin, Dan Gracey, Seung Beom Kim
and the Disney Storybook Artists.

ISBN 978-1-4748-4458-1

Printed in China

Contents

An Unforgettable Family

Dory was a little blue tang. She lived with her parents in a beautiful coral cave surrounded by sea grass.

From a very young age, Dory had trouble remembering things.

"Hi, I'm Dory," she would say when she met someone new, and then she would tell them that she had short-term memory loss.

Dory's parents worried about their forgetful daughter and did everything they could to stop her from getting lost.

But one day, Dory did get lost.

"Just keep swimming, just keep swimming," she sang to herself, getting further and further away from her home.

Time passed and Dory grew up, but she still asked every fish she met if they had seen her parents.

"Where did you see them last?" the fish would ask.

"Well ... uh. Funny story, but, uh ... I forgot."

Poor Dory had forgotten where she came from.

Soon, she forgot about her parents, too.

Dory met a clownfish called Marlin. Kind-hearted Dory helped Marlin find his missing son, Nemo.

A year later, the three friends lived together on the coral reef. They had a happy and colourful home, and had lots of fun.

One day, Dory suddenly muttered something under her breath:
"The Jewel of Morro Bay, California".

Just then, a flood of memories came rushing into her head.
She remembered her parents and her home – she was from California!

"Dory, California's all the way across the ocean," said Marlin.

"Please, Marlin," said Dory. "Please help me find my family."

"Yeah, Dad," said Nemo. "You can get us all the way across the ocean, right?"

Marlin sighed.

Soon the three friends were hitching a ride to California with their old
friend, Crush the turtle.

But when Dory, Marlin and Nemo arrived in Morro Bay, California, disaster struck. Dory was scooped up by a human and carried away in a boat!

"Don't worry, Dory," a panicked Marlin called after her. "Stay calm! We'll come and find you."

Dory was dropped into a tank. An octopus appeared and reached one of his long tentacles towards her. "Name's Hank," he said.

Hank explained that Dory was in Quarantine, and the orange tag clipped to her fin was a transport tag – she was going to be taken to an aquarium in Cleveland.

"Cleveland!" gasped Dory. "No, I can't go to Cleveland! I have to get to the Jewel of Morro Bay, California…."

"That's this place," said Hank. "The Marine Life Institute. This *is* the Jewel of Morro Bay. You're here."

Hank said he would help Dory search for her parents if she gave him her transport tag. He liked the idea of living in a nice, safe tank in Cleveland. Dory agreed, so Hank scooped her up into a coffee pot full of cold water and they set off to explore the institute.

Dory spotted a bucket with the word 'DESTINY' on it. She felt it was very important that she get into that bucket – so she did! Hank followed the bucket as Dory was carried away by a member of staff.

Dory was tipped into a large pool, home to a whale shark called Destiny. Her neighbour was Bailey, a beluga whale. Destiny realized that she had known Dory when they were young! Dory had lived in the Open Ocean exhibit next door and they used to talk to each other through the pipes.

Dory had to get to Open Ocean – that's where her parents would be!

But Dory didn't want to swim through the pipes to the Open Ocean exhibit. She might get lost.

Just then, Dory spotted some pushchairs on the side of Destiny's pool. "We're gonna hijack one of those!" Dory said. She jumped into a small cup of water on the tray of one of the pushchairs.

Hank pushed her across the park to the Open Ocean exhibit and gently dropped Dory into the water. She gave him her orange tag.

"Now go get your family," Hank said.

Dory swam down through the clear, cool tank. At the bottom, she saw a trail of shells. Suddenly, she remembered seeing a similar trail when she was a child. Her parents had made a shell path to guide her back whenever she got lost. But one day, she had got sucked into the pipes and whisked away into the ocean!

This was her home, but where were her parents? There were no blue tangs at all! Dory didn't know what to do.

Just then, a friendly crab appeared. He explained that all the blue tangs had been taken to Quarantine, ready to be driven to the aquarium in Cleveland.

Dory couldn't believe it! She had to get back to Quarantine!

The only way to Quarantine was through the pipes. Dory was nervous, but she swam in. Suddenly, two shapes emerged from the darkness. It was Marlin and Nemo! They had met a bird called Becky who had carried them in a bucket into the institute to search for Dory.

"You found me!" Dory cried. She explained about Hank, Destiny, Bailey and the shell paths. Dory's journey to find her parents would be much easier now that she had her friends with her.

But by the time Dory, Marlin and Nemo
arrived in Quarantine, the tank of blue tangs
had already been loaded on to the lorry heading
for Cleveland!

Luckily, Hank was there to help. He lifted
them in the coffee pot and placed them into
the tank inside the lorry.

The other blue tangs recognized Dory, but
they had sad news ... Dory's parents had left for
Quarantine years ago. Dory was heartbroken.

Slowly, Dory drifted back into the waiting coffee pot. As Hank picked it up and backed out of the lorry, he peered into the pot in alarm.

"Where's everybody else?" he asked Dory. Marlin and Nemo were still in the tank on the lorry!

Before Hank could do anything about it, a worker grabbed him and bundled him back onto the lorry, too. The coffee pot fell to the floor and shattered. Dory spilled into a drain, which took her out into the ocean. Once again, she was lost and alone.

In the bay outside the institute, Dory swam along, wondering
what to do. Then something caught her eye – a trail of shells!
She followed it. Suddenly, two blue tangs appeared. Dory gasped.
It was her parents!

They had been creating shell trails all this time, in the hope that
Dory would see them and remember.

"It's you! It's really you!" cried Dory, bursting into tears.

"Oh, honey, you found us," said Dory's mum. "And you know why
you found us? Because you remembered. You remembered in your
own amazing Dory way."

Dory was so happy ... but she hadn't forgotten her other family,
Marlin and Nemo. She had to save them!

Dory and her parents swam towards the institute's walls. They watched in horror as the lorry started to drive away with Marlin, Nemo and Hank still inside!

Dory swam around in a panic. Then she remembered her friends. "DESTINEEEEEE!" she called in her best whale voice.

"Dory?" Destiny answered. The whale shark leaped over the wall and into the ocean to help her friend. Bailey came too!

The friends swam after the lorry and Destiny used her tail to flip Dory up to it. Inside, Hank helped Dory into the tank containing Marlin and Nemo.

"You came back!" said Nemo.

"Of course," said Dory. "I couldn't leave my family."

Then Marlin had an idea. He called out to Becky the bird. When she arrived, she scooped Marlin and Nemo into her bucket again.

"We don't have Dory!" cried Marlin.

But Becky didn't stop. She flew away and dropped Marlin and Nemo into the ocean.

Dory and Hank were still inside the lorry!

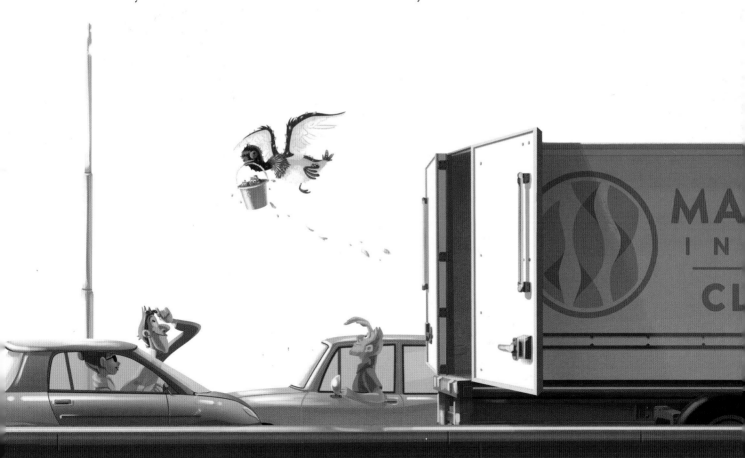

Hank slipped
out of a vent and
spread himself across
the lorry's windscreen.
The shocked driver stopped
the lorry on a bridge and got out.
Hank slipped back inside, climbed into
the driver's seat and locked the doors.
Then he started to drive the lorry!

"Hank," said Dory. "I'm going to ask you to do something crazy."

Hank smiled. He knew what to do.

Dory's family watched in amazement as Hank drove the lorry straight off the bridge – into the ocean! The doors flew open and all the fish spilled out into the sea. They were free!

Dory, Marlin and Nemo headed back home across the ocean, along with all their new family and friends!

Dory was happier than she had ever been. Sometimes she swam off on her own – and she always remembered how to get back to her huge family.

One day, Marlin and Dory were bobbing in the water at the edge of the reef, gazing out into the blue.

"Wow. It really is quite a view," said Marlin.

"Yup," replied Dory.

She turned to Marlin and smiled.

"Unforgettable," she said.

Disney · PIXAR

THE GOOD DINOSAUR

A Long Journey Home

A long time ago, there lived two dinosaurs called Henry and Ida. They lived on a farm next to Clawtooth Mountain. They had three children – Buck, Libby and Arlo.

Arlo was the youngest. From the moment he hatched, he was afraid of everything. Most of all, Arlo was afraid of the wilderness beyond his family's farm.

One day, a critter broke into the farm and ate some corn. Arlo went with his Poppa to look for the critter. But there was a terrifying storm and Henry was swept away by a flooded river. Arlo was devastated – he would never see his Poppa again.

With Poppa gone, the family had to work very hard to keep the farm going. Arlo's Momma was worn out. Arlo helped out by carrying corn on his back.

One day, Arlo caught the critter stealing corn again. As he and the critter fought, they tumbled backwards into the river.

"Momma, Momma!" Arlo cried, but he had been swept too far away for anyone to hear. The river carried Arlo away. Then – *BAM*! The little dinosaur hit his head on a rock and he was pulled under by the current.

When Arlo woke up, he had no idea where he was. The wilderness was all around him.

After a while, the critter appeared. It was a human boy. At first, Arlo was angry with the boy. "This is all your fault!" he shouted.

But the boy brought him berries to eat, and they became friends. Arlo gave the boy a name – Spot.

Spot couldn't talk, so they drew pictures in the dirt to communicate. Arlo learned that, just as he had lost his Poppa, Spot had lost his whole family. The new friends looked up at the moon and let out sad howls together.

The next day, Arlo and Spot met a family of T. rexes called Butch, Ramsey and Nash. They had lost their herd of longhorns.

Arlo offered to help the T. rexes. In return, he asked them if they could show him the way home to Clawtooth Mountain. The T. rexes agreed, so Spot sniffed out the longhorns for them.

But a nasty surprise lay in wait … raptors! This gang of feathery dinosaurs jumped on Butch's back, biting him.

At first, Arlo was frightened and didn't know how to help. But his friend Spot, who was sitting on his back, nudged him. Arlo charged straight at a raptor, head-butting it out of the way. He had done it!

That night, after Arlo, Spot and their new friends had chased the raptors away, they sat around a campfire.

"You and that critter showed real grit today," Butch told Arlo.

The three T. rexes told stories about their adventures, including times when they had fought off other beasts – even crocodiles!

"I'm done being scared," Arlo said.

"Who said I'm not scared?" said Butch.

Arlo was surprised. "But you fought off that croc...."

"Listen, kid," Butch continued, "you can't get rid of fear. But you can get through it. You can find out what you're made of."

The next day, the T. rexes kept their promise to Arlo. They showed him the way to the river that would lead him and Spot home.

The boy and the dinosaur were on their way again. They played and laughed together as they ran along.

Soon, Spot clambered to the top of Arlo's head. As they climbed up the tallest hill, Arlo lifted his head up through the clouds. "Wow," he said.

They could see Clawtooth Mountain. They were heading home!

The next day, the river trail moved into the mountains. Thunder rumbled overhead, the wind blew strongly and it began to rain.

Suddenly, a pack of Pterodactyls swooped down and one of them caught hold of Spot!

"No!" Arlo yelled, trying to grab the boy back. But the Pterodactyl was too strong. With one last tug, the creature took to the sky with Spot grasped in its claws.

"Spot!" Arlo cried as his little friend disappeared.

Arlo chased the Pterodactyls down to the river. As the storm raged
on, he bravely charged at the creatures and finally rescued Spot.

Suddenly, the river burst its banks. Arlo and Spot were swept away by
the flood waters, and they were heading towards a waterfall! The little
dinosaur swam with all his strength. He managed to reach Spot just
before they tumbled over the edge. The two friends clung to each other
as they fell into the river far, far below.

SPLASH! They landed in the river at the bottom of the waterfall. Exhausted, Arlo climbed onto land. He was still holding his little friend.

Arlo and Spot looked at each other and smiled. They were feeling shocked and bruised, but they were okay.

The next morning, the storm had passed. Arlo and Spot set off once more along the river trail.

After a while, they saw something strange up ahead – a human family! Spot ran over to them.

As Arlo watched the family gather around Spot, he knew what he had to do. He had to let Spot go.... It would be better for Spot to live with a family of humans.

The two friends cried as they said goodbye.

For the last part of his journey, Arlo carried on alone.

Finally, the farm came into view.

"Arlo!" cried Momma as she spotted her son.

Buck and Libby came running towards them and
the family laughed and hugged. Arlo was home at last.

INSIDE OUT

Looking After Riley

When a little girl called Riley was born, an Emotion named Joy took control inside Riley's mind. Joy was in charge of a console in Headquarters, and she kept Riley happy.

A golden sphere rolled into Headquarters and Joy picked it up. This was Riley's first memory and it showed her as a baby. It was golden because it was a happy memory.

As Riley grew older, Joy was joined by four more Emotions. Fear helped to keep Riley safe. Once he stopped her from tripping over a power cable.

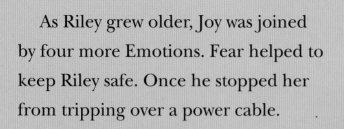

Disgust kept Riley away from things that looked, smelled or tasted funny. Like broccoli!

Anger cared very deeply about things being fair for Riley. When Anger was in charge of the console, Riley often had a tantrum.

Finally, there was Sadness. Like all the Emotions, she wanted to help Riley. But Joy wanted Riley to be happy all the time. How could Sadness help?

When something important happened to Riley, a core memory was created. There were five core memories and each one powered an Island of Personality.

Riley had five islands – Goofball, Friendship, Hockey, Honesty and Family.

When Riley was 11, her mum and dad announced that they were moving from their hometown in Minnesota to San Francisco. The Emotions panicked. How would Riley feel about leaving her home and all her friends?

After a long car journey, Riley looked up at her new home. The Emotions were speechless. The house looked old and dreary.

Joy was determined to keep Riley happy. She drew a circle on the floor around Sadness.

"This is the circle of sadness," Joy told her. "Your job is to make sure that all the sadness stays inside it."

On her first day at her new school, Riley had to stand up and tell the class about herself. She began to share a happy memory about playing hockey. But suddenly, her smile faded.

"You've left the circle!" Joy said to Sadness. "You've touched the hockey memory sphere and turned it blue!"

In class, Riley started to cry, creating the first-ever blue core memory. Joy was furious! She pressed a button, and a tube began to suck away the blue sphere. But the tube also sucked up the other five core memories – as well as Joy and Sadness!

Joy and Sadness were dumped faraway in Riley's mind, but they managed to find their way to Goofball Island. Like all the Islands, it was dark.

"We need to get back to Headquarters," said Joy, "so that these core memories can bring power back to the Islands of Personality!"

Clutching the five memories, Joy began to tiptoe across the light line that led to Headquarters.

"But what if we fall into the Memory Dump?" said Sadness. "We'll be forgotten forever!"

"We won't fall," said Joy. "Just think positive."

Back in Headquarters, Fear, Disgust and Anger were struggling to look after Riley on their own.

When Anger took control of the console, Riley became cross with her dad. When she refused to goof around with him, Goofball Island began to crumble. "Run!" Joy shouted to Sadness. They made it to safety just before the island toppled into the Memory Dump.

Anger was still driving the console as
Riley chatted to her old friend Meg on
her laptop. Meg told Riley about a new
girl on the hockey team. Riley missed
playing hockey with her old friends,
so the news made her angry. She
slammed her laptop shut.

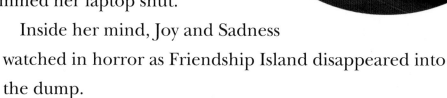

Inside her mind, Joy and Sadness
watched in horror as Friendship Island disappeared into
the dump.

"Goodbye friendship, hello loneliness," said Sadness.

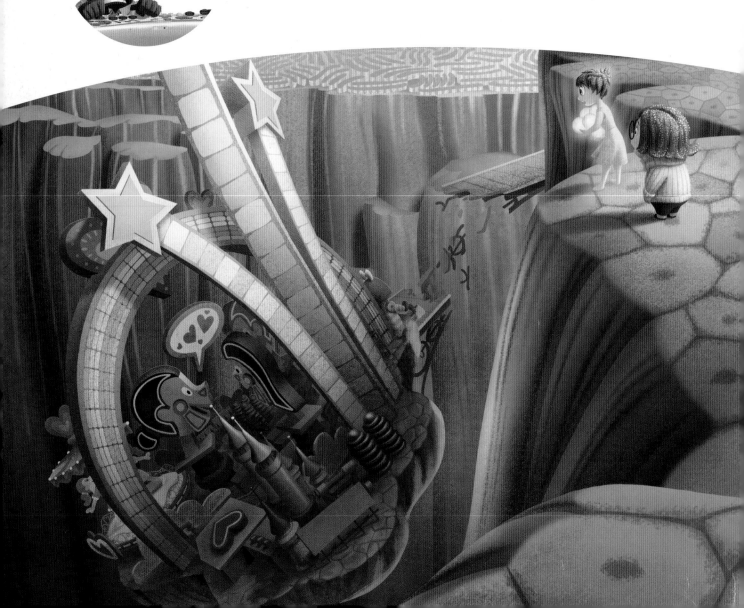

A little while later, Joy and Sadness were walking through Long Term
Memory, where millions and millions of memories were stored on shelves.
They bumped into a funny-looking pink creature with legs like a cat and a
trunk like an elephant.

"Bing Bong!" said Joy excitedly. "You were Riley's imaginary friend!"

Bing Bong decided to travel to Headquarters with the two Emotions.
He danced around happily and gave his bag to Joy to help her carry the
core memories.

Bing Bong led Joy and Sadness to Imagination Land. From there, they hoped to catch the Train of Thought back to Headquarters.

Imagination Land was an amazing place – there was a French Fry Town, a Cloud Town and an Imaginary Boyfriend Generator!

Bing Bong even found his old song-powered rocket wagon, but some Mind Workers threw it into the Memory Dump. As Bing Bong cried sweets, Sadness talked to him about how he felt. Joy was surprised – Sadness helped Bing Bong feel better!

Meanwhile, at Headquarters, Anger decided that Riley should run away – back to Minnesota. As he plugged an idea bulb into the console, the idea popped into Riley's head.

At that moment, Joy and Sadness were on the Train of Thought.

They found a memory sphere they both loved. Sadness remembered Riley being sad because she had lost a hockey match. Joy loved it when the whole team had cheered Riley up.

Later, Riley began planning to run away. Without asking, she took a credit card from Mum's handbag so that she could buy a bus ticket to Minnesota.

Riley's dishonesty caused Honesty Island to collapse. As it crumbled, Joy, Sadness and Bing Bong were thrown from the train.

Soon afterwards, Family Island also began to crumble. Joy fell deep, deep down into the Memory Dump!

At that moment, Riley was heading to the bus station, feeling nothing.

Down in the dump, Joy felt hopeless. She looked again at the hockey memory sphere that she and Sadness had found on the train. Suddenly Joy realized that Sadness was important – Riley's friends had come to help because she was sad.

Just then, Bing Bong appeared. The pair decided to fly out of the Memory Dump in Bing Bong's rocket wagon.

They sang loudly to power the rocket, but each time they flew up, they couldn't quite reach the top of the cliff.

When they gave it one last try, Bing Bong jumped out without Joy noticing. Now the wagon was light enough and Joy flew up to the cliff top. When she looked back, she saw Bing Bong waving to her from the dump far below.

Joy spotted Sadness floating away on a cloud. "I only make everything worse!" Sadness was saying. Joy had to reach her.

Using the Imaginary Boyfriend Generator, she made a tall tower of boyfriends. Joy climbed up it and swung towards Sadness.

"Gotcha!" Joy cried as she grabbed her in mid-air. "Hang on!"

The two flew through the air towards Headquarters. Joy was still clutching the bag of core memories.

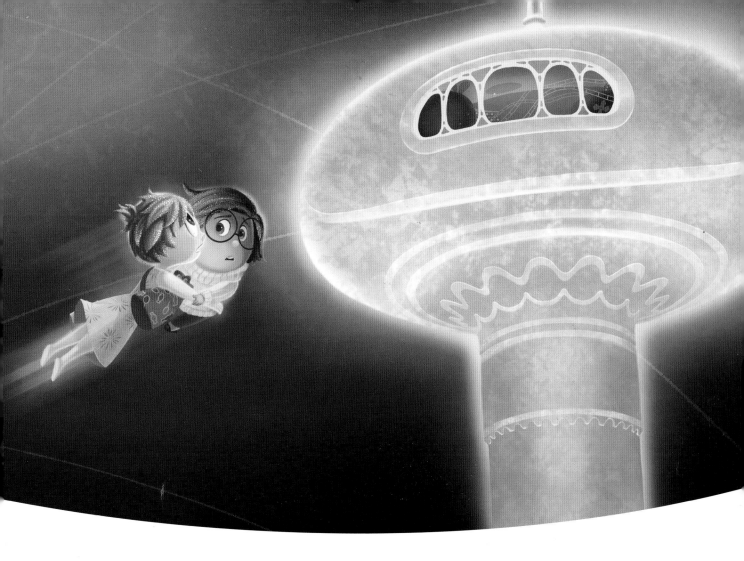

Back in Headquarters, Fear, Disgust and Anger were relieved to see the two Emotions return.

Joy let Sadness take control of the console.

On the bus, Riley suddenly felt very sad.

"Wait!" she called out to the driver. "I want to get off!"

When Riley arrived back at home, her mind filled with memories of her old friends and her old home. She began to cry. Her memories made her feel sad because Joy had given all the golden core memories to Sadness. The spheres had turned blue!

Riley told her parents how she felt and they gave her a big hug. She began to feel better.

A few days later, the Islands of Personality had reappeared. Joy, Sadness, Anger, Fear and Disgust were excited about the future. After all, Riley was 12 now ... what could happen?

MONSTERS, INC.

Mike's Laughing Matter

BEEP! BEEP! BEEP! Mike Wazowski's eye popped open. He stretched his arms and grinned. It was time for work! He turned off his alarm clock and hopped out of bed. He didn't want to be late for his job at Monsters, Inc. Mike took his work very seriously.

When Mike arrived at work, he headed straight to the locker room.
His job was to go into the human world and make kids laugh.
He collected the laughs and brought them back to Monsters, Inc.
Then the company changed the laughs into energy to create power
for the city of Monstropolis.

Mike wasn't just any employee. He was the top laugh collector!
He was always coming up with new jokes.

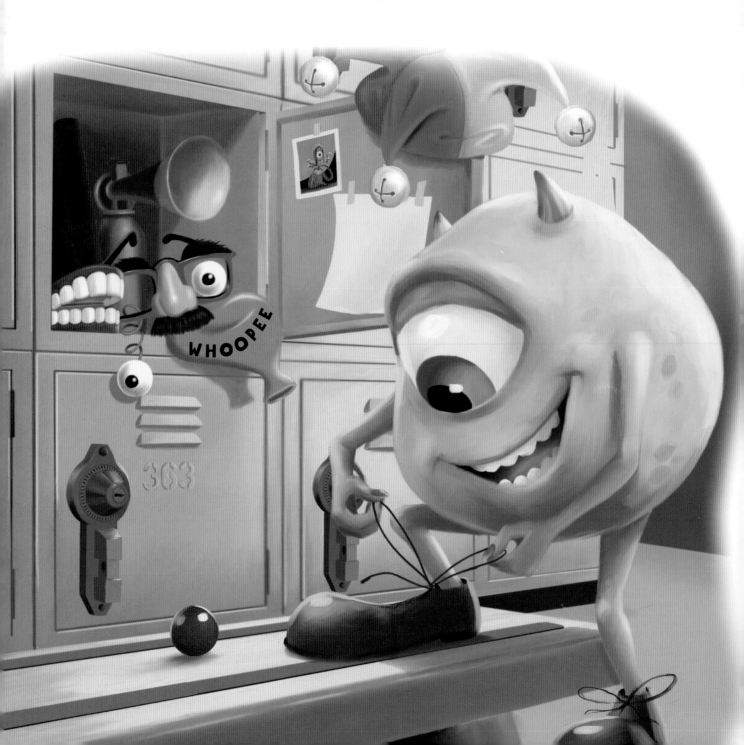

As Mike walked down the hall to the Laugh Floor, a furry orange monster named George waved. "Hi, Mike! Got any plans for the weekend?"

Mike just nodded and kept walking. He didn't have time to chat if he was going to run through his routine. A moment later, he arrived at his station.

Mike practised his jokes aloud. "A sandal bumped into a sneaker. 'Want to hang out?' the sandal asked. The sneaker raced off. 'Sorry – gotta run!'"

Just then, a door dropped down from the ceiling into his station. "Time to rock and roll!" Mike said excitedly.

Mike walked through the door and into a child's bedroom cupboard. He peeked out. To his surprise, the bedroom was dark and the shades were down. The glow of a night-light filled the room.

Mike tiptoed to the bed. A little boy lay sound asleep under the covers.

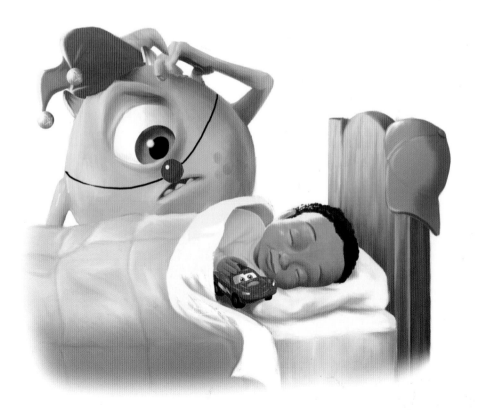

Mike knew he wouldn't be collecting any laughs here. *It seems pretty early for bedtime*, he thought, stepping back through the cupboard door into Monsters, Inc. He looked over at his empty laugh canister. "Guess the kid had a busy day. Oh, well. I'll just have to crack up someone else tonight."

A moment later, a new door slid down and Mike stepped through it. "You've got to be kidding!" he whispered, his eye wide.

His audience – a young girl – was asleep. She was even snoring!

"I'm not going to give up," Mike declared. After all, he *was* the funniest monster at Monsters, Inc. Mike took a deep breath, returned to the Laugh Floor and tried another door. Then another. No luck.

All the children he visited were asleep!

"What a terrible day," Mike grumbled as he walked back through his station door yet again. Then he packed up his belongings.

Outside Monsters, Inc., a few monsters were talking with Sulley, the president of the company and Mike's best friend. Mike went over and told his friends what had happened.

"Doesn't anyone stay up past dinner?" he asked.

George shrugged his furry orange shoulders. "I didn't have any problems."

"I collected nearly a dozen canisters," said Charlie, a skinny green monster. "One of my best days ever."

Sulley patted Mike's arm. "Probably just a coincidence, pal. I'm sure tomorrow will be better. Why don't you come have dinner with us?"

Mike shook his head. He needed to go home and write some more jokes. He was determined to have the most laughs that week.

When Mike got home, his phone was ringing. It was his girlfriend, Celia. "How was work?" she asked.

"Terrible," Mike said. "I didn't even fill up one canister!"

"Don't worry," Celia told him. "You're the funniest monster I know. The laughs will come. So, do you want to go to a movie on Saturday?"

"Can I let you know tomorrow?" Mike asked.

"Sure," Celia replied.

Mike hung up the phone. He wrote eight new jokes, re-read them several times and then hurried off to bed.

The next day, Mike was bursting with excitement. "What did the ghost serve at his birthday party? I-*scream*!" he joked, warming up.

But it happened again. Each time Mike stepped through a closet door, he found a sleeping child. What was going on?

Mike stomped back to the Laugh Floor. This was nothing to laugh about. His reputation as the funniest monster at Monsters, Inc. was on the line.

"What's the matter, Mike?" George asked. "You look cranky."

"Wanna grab a bite?" Sulley suggested.

Other monsters had started to look at Mike, wondering what was going on.

"Not now," Mike said, pacing back and forth. "This is a disaster."

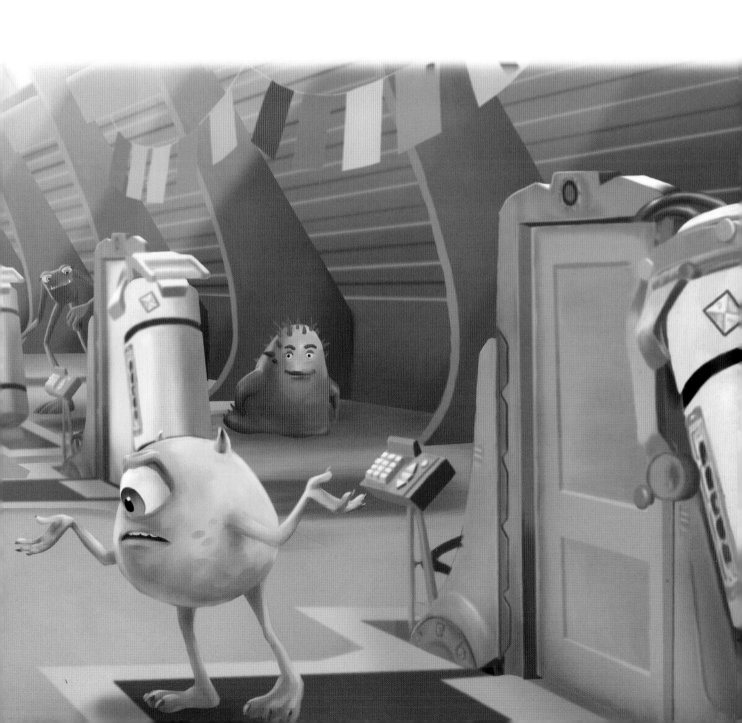

"Maybe you're losing your touch," George said.

"Maybe you should get more sleep," Charlie advised.

Mike felt his face getting hot. "Listen –"

Suddenly Mike noticed that Sulley was grinning. And so were the other monsters. Even Celia's hair snakes were smiling!

"Maybe you shouldn't take your laughs so seriously," Sulley suggested with a wink.

"What do you know about this?" Mike asked, suspicious.

"We got you!" George yelled. He and Charlie high-fived.

"Got me?" Mike said, giving everyone a one-eyed stare.

"The guys thought it was time to help you lighten up and laugh a bit more, Mike," Sulley explained. "When was the last time you went to lunch with one of us? You haven't stopped to chat in weeks. And I heard Celia asked you to the movies on Saturday?"

"But – I – I mean, work has been –" Mike tried to explain that he took his jokes very seriously. Then he realized his friends were right. He had been trying so hard to collect laughs that he'd forgotten to have some of his own! He smiled. "Okay, how'd you do it?" he asked.

"When you weren't home, I snuck into your house and changed your clock," Charlie told him. "That's why the kids were all asleep when you walked into their bedrooms."

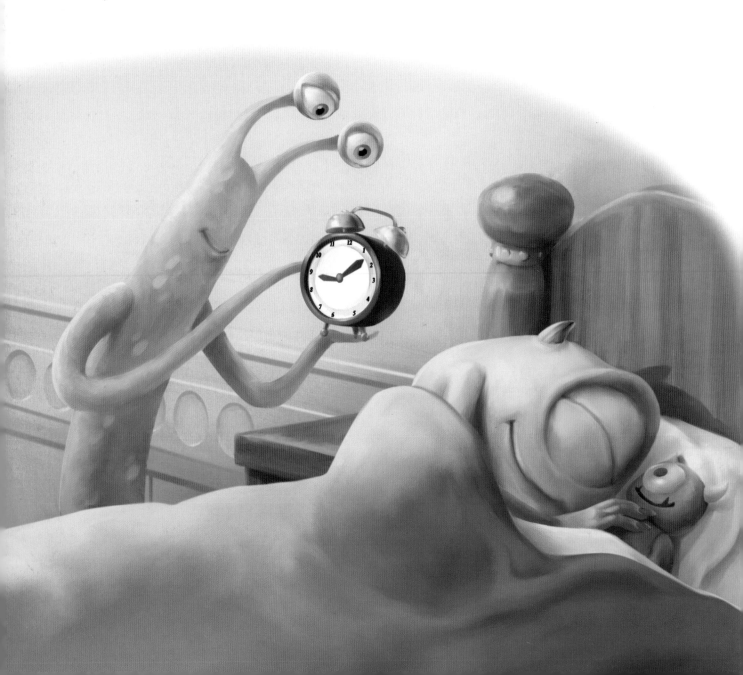

As Mike looked at all the smiling monster faces around him, he realized how much his friends cared about him. He found himself finally beginning to relax. Then he let out a loud chuckle.

Soon everyone on the Laugh Floor was cracking up.

"I have to admit it – you guys really had me going,"

Mike said, wiping a happy tear from his eye.

Sulley grinned. "This time, the joke was on you!"

The Search for the Perfect Gift

It was Queen Atta's birthday and everyone on Ant Island had spent a whole week collecting gifts. The queen sat on her grassy throne as each ant presented a gift to her.

"Oh, what a lovely berry!" Queen Atta exclaimed at the first present. "It's so shiny and red."

"I picked the biggest one I could find," an ant explained.

Other ants brought pinecones, seeds, grain and more treats.

There was one ant, however, who didn't have a gift yet. His name was Flik.
He was a clumsy but brilliant inventor, and he had a big crush on Queen Atta.
He told Princess Dot, Atta's sister, about his present problem.

"It can't be just any gift. It has to be the *perfect* gift," Flik explained.

"But Atta will like whatever you give her," Dot told him.

Flik shook his head. "Atta is the queen now, so whatever I give her has to be worthy of royalty."

"I'm sure we will think of something if we work together," Dot suggested.

Flik smiled. "That would be great, Dot. Thank you."

So the two friends set out to look for the perfect gift. They looked high, and they looked low. They looked under leaves and over toadstools.

Suddenly, Dot cried out in excitement. "Look! I found a four-leaf clover!"

Flik ran over. Unfortunately, when they both examined it more closely, it was only a three-leaf clover.

"Sorry, Flik," said Dot.

"Don't worry about it," Flik said with smile. "We'll find something."

But *something* found them first! A hungry frog poked his head through the grass.

"LOOK OUT!" Flik cried.

Luckily, Flik and Dot escaped from the big frog. They took cover in a nearby patch of flowers.

"Now what?" asked Dot.

Flik thought and thought. Then he spotted a daisy, and an idea started to bloom.

"It's just a plain, old daisy now," he explained to Dot. "But soon it will be a merry-go-round for Atta!"

"Are you sure, Flik?" Dot asked, uncertain. Although Flik was very smart, his inventions often went wrong.

Flik nodded. "Absolutely," he replied. "This is going to be great!"

Dot smiled. "Okay. How can I help?"

"You can be the very first passenger," said Flik. "Hop on."

But the ants soon realized that the daisy spun way too fast!

"Whoa!" cried Dot.

"Whoops," Flik said. "Sorry about that!"

"That's okay," Dot told Flik. She still believed in him.

Within a few minutes, Flik had a brand-new idea.

"Maybe Atta could use a nice, cool breeze," he said. He placed a strong piece of grass around the daisy's stem. He would use the flower as a fan. "Get ready to chill, Dot!"

Dot sat down across from Flik and the daisy. "Okay, GO!" she shouted, and Flik gave a great big tug.

Poor Dot! The wind from the daisy spinner sent the little ant high into the air.

Dot beat her wings as fast as she could. She landed safely on the flower's stem.

Flik scratched his head. "Finding the perfect gift is really hard!"

"Maybe you should just get Atta a card," Dot suggested.

"I will not give up!" Flik declared. He began pacing back and forth, racking his brain for ideas.

"I'll build her a beach umbrella," he said aloud.

"She has one already," Dot reminded him.

"How about a sprinkler?" asked Flik. "If I just find a source of water to funnel into...."

Dot smiled and shook her head. Flik sure was a determined inventor!

Just then, Queen Atta walked by.

"Hello, Dot. Hello, Flik," she said. Then she noticed the fallen flower next to Flik. "Is that for me?"

Flik looked at the ground and answered in a quiet voice. "Well, not really. It's just a plain, old daisy."

"There's nothing plain about it," said Queen Atta. "I think it's perfect."

Dot grinned. "Me, too!"

"Happy birthday, Atta," Flik and Dot said.

Atta smiled. "Thank you. And thank you both for a perfect birthday present!"

Flik sat down next to Queen Atta. He realized that she was right: the daisy made the perfect gift, for it was a gift they could all enjoy together.

Radiator Springs Road Trip

It had been an exciting afternoon in Radiator Springs. Lightning McQueen had just been on TV talking about the big Piston Cup tie-breaker race.

"Do you think he can beat Chick Hicks?" Sally the blue sports car asked.

"Lightning can beat anybody!" shouted Mater the tow truck. "I sure wish we were there to cheer him on."

"Well," said Doc, the town judge and doctor, "I've been thinking about that. Maybe we should head on out there. He's still a rookie. He needs us."

All of Lightning's friends hit the road – and the road to California was a long one. To keep from getting tired in the hot sun, the cars pulled over at a rest stop.

Flo looked around and smiled. "I love Radiator Springs, but it sure is nice to take a trip from time to time!"

After resting for a while, the cars went on their way. Mater was leading the line. When he turned around to check on his friends, he didn't see Guido the forklift. Worried, Mater went to look for him. He found Guido at the end of the line. It was hot, and the little forklift had fallen behind. Mater offered to give him a tow.

"I hope you don't mind lookin' at where we've been instead of where we're going," Mater said.

Finally, the Radiator Springs gang arrived at the Los Angeles International Speedway. It was almost race time! Sarge took command. "Flo, oil stand over here. Guido, tyres and tools right there."

"Pit stop!" Guido shouted.

Ramone was itching to do some painting.

"Try snazzing up this pit. We need to show off our star car," Doc suggested.

"Where is Lightning?" Mater wondered aloud.

"Come on, Mater," said Doc. "Let's find the kid."

There were so many cars around that Doc and Mater had trouble spotting Lightning.

"There he is!" Mater shouted. "Over there!"

Doc turned to look, but Lightning was already gone. Determined to find his friend, Mater began a search of his own. "Lightning McQueen!" Mater shouted. "Where you at, buddy?"

Mater spotted the tent for Rust-eze, Lightning's racing sponsor. Maybe Lightning was in there. Inside, Mater found himself surrounded by rusty cars.

"Hey, you're Tow Mater!" said an old van. "Lightning's pal. We've heard about you."

"How about a free sample, Mater?" said a grinning blue car. "It will take some of that rust off your bumper."

"Rust? On me? *Where?*" Mater asked, alarmed.

Just then, Flo rushed in and took Mater away.

"Come back soon!" the rusty cars called.

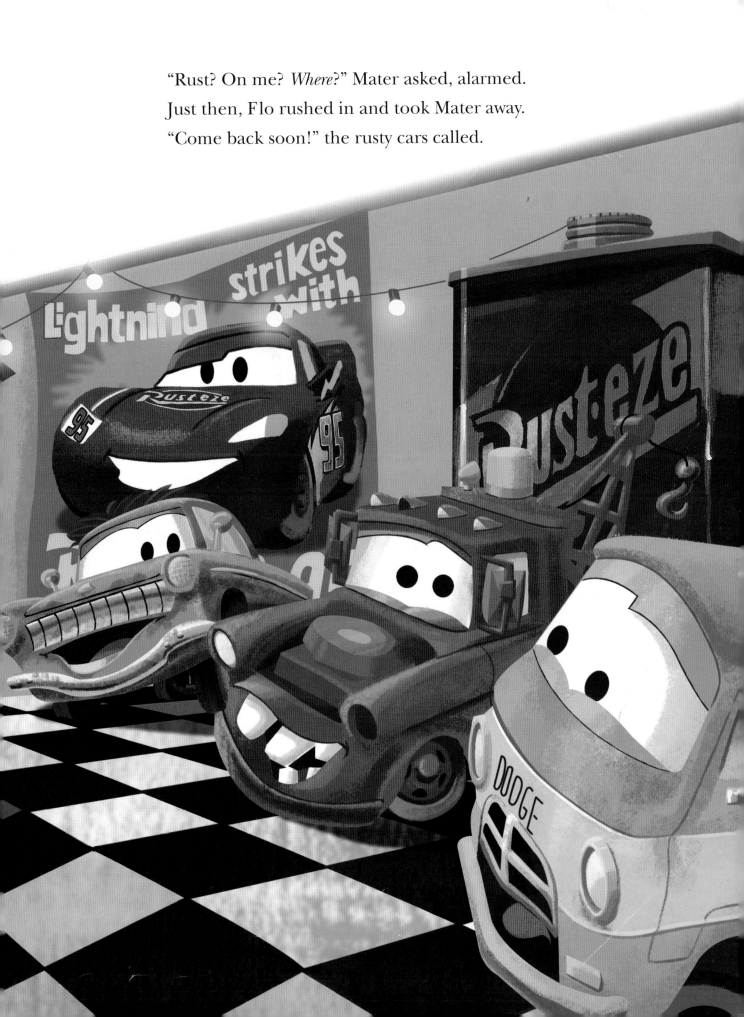

"Let's look for some decorations for Lightning's pit area!"
Flo suggested to Mater.

Forgetting what he was *actually* looking for, Mater followed
Flo to a truck that was selling lots of cool stuff.

Mater picked out some snazzy antenna balls.

"Ooh, I like those," Flo said. Then she added some yellow banners that matched Lightning's team colours.

"Looks like we're going to have a *ball* today," Mater joked.

Flo laughed. "Good one, Mater," she said.

Meanwhile, Doc had gone to the other side of the track to check out the competing crews. As he neared Chick Hicks's tent, he heard something bad. Very bad.

"I'm winning this time, no matter what I have to do," Chick told his crew. "I'm going to force The King and that smart-alecky rookie off the track. The Cup is mine, boys."

Doc knew he had to warn Lightning that Chick was up to his usual dirty tricks. But where was Lightning?

Doc found Mater and told him about Chick's plan.

"We gotta warn Lightning!" yelled Mater.

"This area is for press only," said a tough-looking SUV guard.

"Hey, that's Doc Hudson you're talking to!" Mater said.

The guard stood his ground. "No one gets through – and that's final!"

Doc turned away. It looked like he wasn't going to get to Lightning in time. "Sorry to let you down, kid," he said quietly.

Mater didn't like seeing Doc look so sad. What could he do to cheer him up? "Here, Doc, this is for you," Mater said, tossing Doc one of the antenna balls. "It has Lightning's number on it. We're part of his team. He needs us!"

Doc grinned. "You're right, Mater. We came here to help our friend, and that's exactly what we're going to do!"

Mater spun around and let out a holler. "*Whoo-ee!* Here we come, Lightning!" he yelled.

"Let's get to the pit," Doc said. "And tell Ramone I need a special paint job, Mater!"

This is what friendship is all about, Doc thought, as he drove up to the crew-chief platform. The crowd roared as Doc stood there proudly. Ramone finished painting the blazing words on Doc's side: FABULOUS HUDSON HORNET.

As Lightning made a turn around the track, he saw his Radiator Springs friends in the pit-crew area. They had come all the way to California to cheer him on!

"Hey, kid, keep an eye on Hicks," Doc said over his radio headset. "He's up to no good."

But Lightning wasn't worried. He knew that Doc and Mater and all his friends were looking out for him. Newly energized, Lightning revved his motor and took off down the racetrack. *KA-CHOW!*

THE INCREDIBLES
A Super Family

Once upon a time, a group of people called the Supers were loved by everyone around the world. The Supers had special powers that they used to keep the world safe from evil.

One of these Supers was especially good at his job. His name was Mr Incredible, and he was Super strong. He sometimes worked with Elastigirl. She could stretch her arms and legs Super far and catch a criminal from down the block!

But then times changed. People stopped wanting to be saved, and they turned against the Supers. The Supers had to quit being heroes. They went into hiding, pretending to be normal people with normal lives.

Mr Incredible and Elastigirl were known as Mr and Mrs Parr. They had a son named Dash, a daughter named Violet and a baby named Jack-Jack. They tried to act like a typical family, but sometimes that was difficult – because the kids had Super powers, too! Dash could run Super fast and Violet could turn invisible and create force fields. Baby Jack-Jack's powers had not yet been discovered.

Outside the house, the kids had to keep their powers a secret. But inside the house, they used their Super powers for better or worse – even at the dinner table!

Then one day, Mr Parr opened his briefcase to find a strange computer inside. A woman's face appeared on the screen.

"Hello, Mr Incredible," the woman said. "My name is Mirage. A highly experimental prototype robot has escaped our control." Mirage asked Mr Incredible to take on the mission of stopping the robot. "The Supers aren't gone, Mr Incredible. *You're* still here."

Mr Incredible was thrilled to be able to act as a Super again. Without telling his family, he headed to the secret island of Nomanisan, where he swiftly defeated the robot.

After that, Mr Incredible was called to do more Super work. He accomplished every mission … until one. This time, Mr Incredible faced the most powerful robot yet. He tried every Super move he knew, but the robot was better, faster and stronger.

Suddenly, a stranger wearing a Super suit appeared. "It's too much for Mr Incredible!" the stranger yelled, laughing evilly.

Mr Incredible realized that the person who controlled the robots was actually a villain named Syndrome.

"Who's Super *now*?" Syndrome shouted as he trapped Mr Incredible.

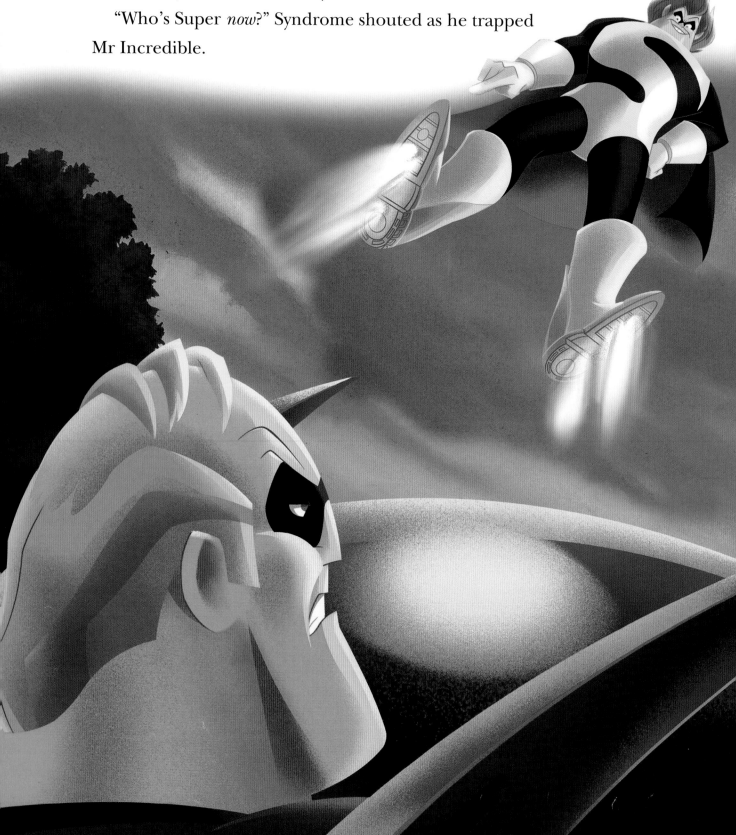

Meanwhile, Mrs Parr had figured out that her husband was working as a Super again. Using a tracking device, she saw that Mr Incredible was on Nomanisan. She knew he was in trouble, so Mrs Parr put on her Super suit and transformed into Elastigirl, ready to rescue her husband.

Dash and Violet couldn't just stay at home while their parents were in danger. They put on their Super suits and joined their mum.

The family raced to Nomanisan. They fought Syndrome's guards, then they freed Mr Incredible. Violet and Dash had never really seen Elastigirl and Mr Incredible in action before. They were awesome!

Suddenly, Syndrome arrived. Using his immobi-ray, the villain trapped the Incredibles in a force field.

"Looks like I've hit the jackpot!" Syndrome cackled. He told them his evil plan: he would send his own robot to attack the city. Then, when all hope was lost, he would appear and defeat the robot himself. He would look like the most powerful Super of all.

"I'll be a bigger hero than you ever were!" Syndrome yelled. Then he flew off.

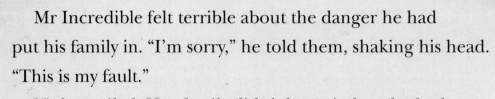

Mr Incredible felt terrible about the danger he had
put his family in. "I'm sorry," he told them, shaking his head.
"This is my fault."

Violet smiled. Her family didn't know it, but she had
protected herself with her own force field. She made her
way to the control panel and freed everyone. The Incredibles
were back and ready to rescue!

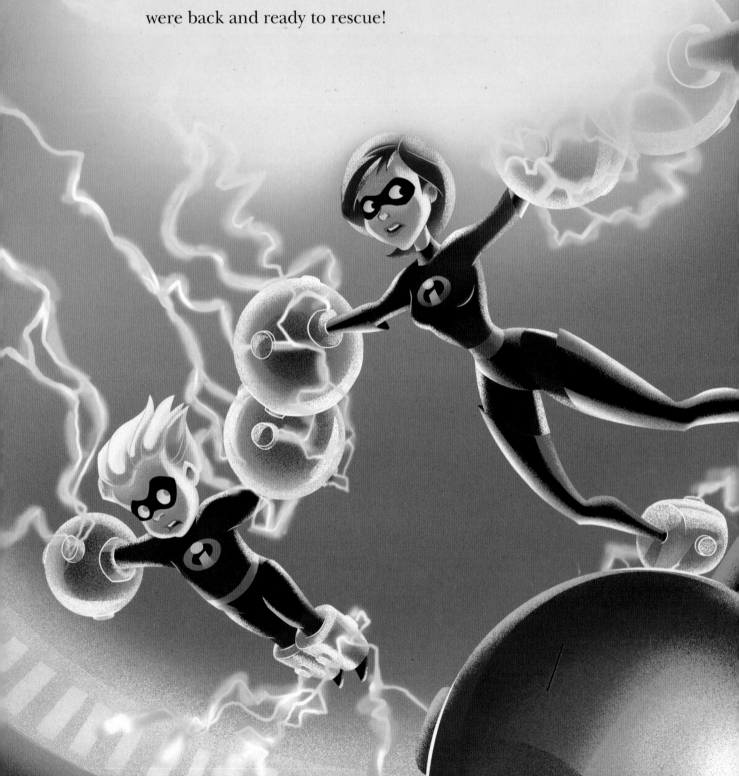

In the city, the robot was on the attack. Syndrome pretended to fight the giant robot using a remote control. People cheered for him. His plan was working!

Then the robot figured out that Syndrome was controlling its every move. It shot a laser ray at Syndrome and the remote flew from the villain's hand.

The Incredibles raced towards the robot.

The family – and their Super friend Frozone – put their powers together to battle fire and ice and the robot's nonstop attacks. Finally, the Incredibles defeated Syndrome's invention. The crowd cheered for the Super family.

After that, the Parr family continued pretending to be normal.
But they all knew that when a villain threatened the world,
the Incredibles would be there to save the day!

Toy Story

A New Mission

Andy was leaving for college, and his toys were heading to the attic. But Sarge and his Green Army Men had a different plan. They climbed up onto the windowsill.

"Hey, Sarge! What are you doing?" asked Buzz.

"War's over, folks," Sarge replied. "We're moving on."

Sarge explained that their tour of duty in Andy's room was complete. It was time he and his troops took up a new mission.

With one final salute, Sarge and his men jumped off the windowsill. They opened their parachutes and flew across the city. Operation New Home was a go!

The three army men landed near a toy store – the perfect place to find a child. Before long, the soldiers spotted a boy and his mother walking towards them.

"This child is military material," Sarge whispered.
"On your marks, gentlemen. Go! Go! Go!"

He and his men jumped into the mother's shopping bag.

But the soldiers weren't taken home for playtime. The mother made a stop at a bakery.

As the boy reached for a giant cookie, he knocked one of the shopping bags over. The army men tumbled to the floor.

After the boy left, the baker spotted the toys. He picked them up and took them into the kitchen, delighted at what he thought were new cake decorations.

After giving them a good wash, the baker placed the Green Army
Men on a birthday cake. Then he put the cake in the refrigerator.

"Looks like we're in for a long, cold night," Sarge said with a sigh.

As soon as morning came, the soldiers were placed in a box and
carried out of the door. They were on the move again!

When the lid of the cake box was finally lifted, Sarge and his men discovered that they were in the middle of a birthday party.

"Green Army Men! Cool!" exclaimed the birthday boy. He plucked the soldiers off the cake and set them aside.

"This could be it, men," whispered Sarge. "This boy could lead us to our new home!"

The soldiers nodded in agreement. Their mission was back on track!

The soldiers watched as the boy enjoyed his party.
But then, somehow, they lost sight of him.

Sarge scanned the room. "Target is heading for the exit.
Let's move, move, *move!*"

The army men followed the boy out of the front door.
But they were too late. He was gone.

Before the Green Army Men could retreat, a pizza delivery lorry screeched to a stop near them. The driver honked his horn.

A waiter came out of the restaurant carrying a stack of pizza boxes. "It's about time," he grumbled to the driver. "Take these to the Wilderness Explorer picnic. There are a lot of hungry kids waiting for lunch!"

Sarge looked at his men and smiled. Then they climbed onto the lorry.

The lorry weaved in and out of traffic. Suddenly it hit a bump, causing one of the cadet's parachutes to open. Sarge grabbed on to the soldier as he began to lift off the roof of the lorry. The other soldier held on to Sarge.

The wind was strong. They couldn't hold on much longer.

"Go on without me!" the cadet called out.

But Sarge knew better. "A good soldier never leaves a man behind."

All three soldiers flew off the lorry and landed on the side of the road.

As night fell, the soldiers made a tent out of newspaper. The cadets went to bed, but Sarge stayed awake, wondering when – and where – they would find their new home.

The next morning, the unit awoke to a loud rumble.
Their makeshift shelter was lifted into the air and then
tossed into a rubbish bin – with Sarge still inside!

Sarge looked down to see his soldiers safe in the bushes below.
Then he was thrown into the back of a bin lorry.

The bin man hopped aboard his lorry. Then he drove off.

Sarge struggled to keep his head above the rubbish.
Just as he was about to sink beneath the plastic bags,
he looked up and saw his cadets. They had come to his rescue!

Working together, the other soldiers lowered themselves
into the bin lorry. Sarge reached out and grabbed the hand
of one of the cadets.

"Never leave a man behind, sir," the soldier said.

The troop jumped off the lorry and landed in an alley. Sarge looked at his tired troops and sighed. Maybe leaving Andy's house wasn't such a good idea, after all.

At that moment, the men heard laughter coming from the other side of a wall. They climbed up and peered over. Sarge gasped.

Below them was a beautiful playground. Could this be their new home? They parachuted over for a closer look.

A group of toys greeted the soldiers with open arms. "Welcome to Sunnyside Daycare!"

Ken and Barbie gave the troops a tour of the playground and classrooms. Everything was new and improved now that their old boss, Lotso, wasn't there anymore.

Sarge pulled his men aside and explained that Sunnyside felt like the home they were looking for. The cadets agreed.

The next morning, Sarge proudly watched his men experience
a full day of play at Sunnyside. The troops were finally home.
Mission accomplished!

The Ghost-Light Fish

"Have a great day, Nemo!" Marlin the clownfish said as he hugged his son goodbye. He and Dory, a blue tang fish, were dropping Nemo off at school.

"All right!" Nemo exclaimed. "I will … just as soon as you let go."

Marlin realized he was still hugging his son. "Oh, right!" Marlin said with a chuckle. He let go.

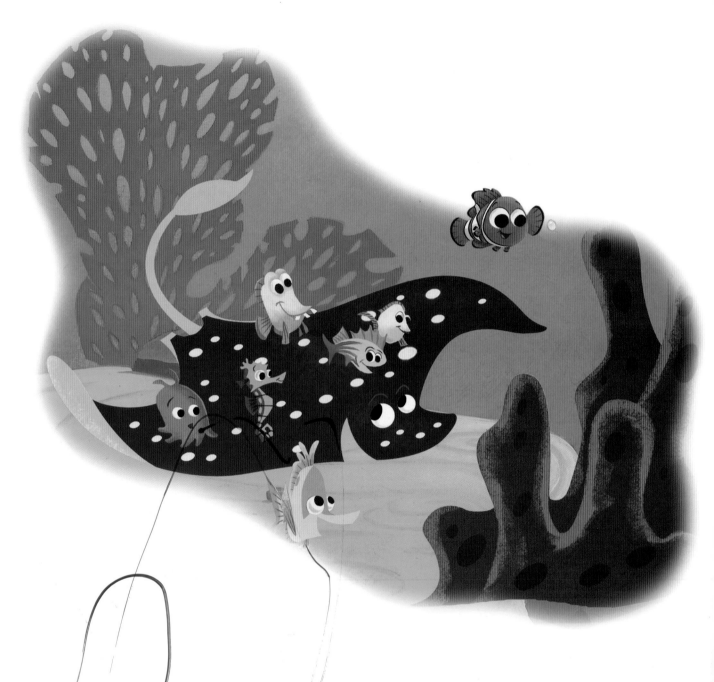

Nemo swam off to join the other students and their teacher, Mr Ray.

"Bye, Dad!" the little clownfish called out. "Bye, Dory! See you later!"

Nemo loved school. So did his friends, Tad the long-nosed butterfly fish, Pearl the octopus and Sheldon the sea horse. How could they not when Mr Ray made everything so much fun?

Mr Ray took his students exploring all over the reef.
Every day, Nemo and his classmates got an up-close look
at different kinds of sea life.

That day, Mr Ray was taking them to a clearing on the
ocean floor.

"Okay, explorers," Mr Ray said when they arrived, "now it's time to do a little searching on your own. Let's see if each of you can find a shell. Then we'll identify them together!"

The youngsters fanned out. Nemo searched in the shadow of some coral. Pearl peeked into a bit of algae. Sheldon dug in the sand.

Tad was the first of Nemo's friends to find something. "Hey, guys!" he cried. "Look at this!"

Nemo, Pearl and Sheldon swam over to their friend.

They crowded around and stared in wonder at the gleaming white shell Tad held in his fin.

"*Coooool,*" said Sheldon.

"It's so pretty," Pearl said admiringly. "Where did you find it?"

Tad pointed to a cave. "In there," he said. "Maybe there are more!" Tad darted towards the cave entrance.

"Yeah!" said Pearl, following him. "I want to find one, too."

"Me, too!" cried Sheldon. "Are you coming, Nemo?" he asked.
"Nah," Nemo replied. "You guys go on." He wanted to find a
shell that was different from everybody else's.

Only a few minutes passed before Nemo heard an odd noise. He looked up and saw Sheldon, Tad and Pearl bolting out of the cave at full speed, screaming loudly.

"What's the matter?" Nemo asked. "Is it a barracuda? An eel?"

Sheldon shook his head. "No, worse!" he said fearfully. "It's a *g-g-ghost fish*!"

"Yeah, right," Nemo replied. Then he noticed Tad's fin was empty. "Where's your shell?" he asked.

Tad looked down. "Aw, shucks," he said, disappointed. "I was going to give it to my mum." Then he peered into the cave. "I must have dropped it in there. But I'm not going back for it. Not with that ghost fish on the loose!"

"Don't worry," Nemo told Tad. "I'll find your shell."

The little clownfish swam bravely into the cave.

See? he thought to himself. *Nothing to be afraid of.*

Just then, Nemo froze. On the cave wall next to him was a huge, fish-shaped shadow!

Nemo took a deep breath. "Uh, excuse me, Mr Ghost Fish? Or is it Ms Ghost Fish?"

"A ghost fish?!" a tiny voice said nervously. "Where? Where? Don't let it get me!"

The ghost fish didn't *sound* very scary. Nemo swam closer to the shadow. "Are *you* afraid of ghost fish?" he asked it.

"Yeah!" squeaked the little voice. "Who isn't?"

Nemo followed the voice. There, cowering behind a rock, was a little fish, glowing softly with pale orange light.

The ghost fish wasn't a ghost fish at all! It was just a glow-in-the-dark fish. Its glow was shining on an oddly shaped piece of coral and making a spooky-looking shadow!

Nemo's fear was forgotten.

"Oh, hi!" he called out.

Startled, the glowing fish darted behind another rock.
Then, timidly, he peeked out from behind it to study Nemo.

"Don't be afraid," Nemo said. "I'm just a little fish – like you."
He smiled. "My name's Nemo. What's yours?"

The fish swam out cautiously. "Eddy," he replied, his
eyes still wide. "You mean there's no ghost fish?"

Nemo chuckled. "I thought *you* were the ghost fish!"
He explained the whole funny story.

"By the way," said Nemo, "how do you glow like that?"

Eddy shrugged. "I just do," he replied. "My whole family does."

Nemo thought of someone who would know more about Eddy's glow: Mr Ray! So Nemo invited Eddy to meet his teacher and his friends. Then, swimming out of the cave together, the two little fish laughed about the way they had met.

"You really thought *I* was a ghost fish?" Eddy asked with a giggle.

Outside, Nemo rejoined his friends. "Sorry I didn't find your shell," Nemo said to Tad. "But I did find your ghost fish!"

Then Nemo and Eddy told their tale. Before long, the ghost fish was forgotten. Instead, everyone wanted to know more about Eddy!

"Can you glow different colours?" Pearl asked.

"How come the water doesn't put out your light?" questioned Tad.

Nemo wanted to know what made Eddy glow.

"Good question, Nemo," Mr Ray replied. "See these patches on either side of Eddy's jaw? Inside them are teeny-tiny glow-in-the-dark organisms. When you see Eddy glow, you're really seeing those organisms glowing."

Everyone *ooohed* and *aaahed* over Eddy's glow patches.

"If you think that's cool," said Eddy, "you should meet the rest of my family!"

Eddy led the whole class into the cave to show them his glow-in-the-dark world – including his family. Nemo thought it was one of the most beautiful things he had ever seen. But there was still one thing weighing on his mind.

"Mr Ray," Nemo whispered to his teacher, "I didn't finish the assignment. I mean, I didn't find a shell."

Mr Ray laughed. "That's okay, Nemo," he replied. "I'd say you still get an 'A' in exploring for today!"

Mixed Signals

The toys were buzzing with excitement. Bonnie was going to the park with Woody the cowboy, Jessie the cowgirl and Dolly. The others were looking forward to a day of play in Bonnie's room.

Only Jessie was worried. "Keep an eye on Buzz," she whispered to her friends. "He's been acting funny. I think he may have a loose wire."

"No problem-o, Jessie," said Hamm the piggy bank.

Moments later, Bonnie rushed into her room. "This is going to be so much fun!" she said, grabbing her backpack. "Buzz, you're in charge now," Bonnie said to the space ranger on her way out. "Keep things under control, okay?"

As soon as the coast was clear, the Peas-in-a-Pod began bouncing on their shelf.

"Let's play!" they shouted.

Buzz stood up. "Wait!" he said. "This looks dangerous."

"What did you say, Buzz?" Slinky Dog asked. But suddenly, he slipped. Slinky Dog plunged over the edge of his shelf, causing an avalanche of aliens and peas.

Squeak, squeak, plunk, plunk, plunk! They tumbled on top of Buzz!

Buzz stood up again. He looked around. "Donde esta mi nave?" he asked.

"Great," Mr Potato Head observed. "The return of Señor Space Nut."

"Yup," Hamm agreed. "He's definitely switched into Spanish mode. Rex, see if you can find any loose wires in his back panel. We've got to fix this."

But as Rex reached for Buzz, the space ranger ran away.

"Catch him!" shouted Hamm, leading the other toys.

Buzz grabbed a curtain from the doll's house and held it up like a bullfighter's cape. As the others surrounded him, Buzz flapped the curtain wildly.

"Buzz, hold on," Slinky Dog said calmly. "You're not yourself."

"I'll grab that curtain before he hits someone in the noggin!" Hamm said as he ran to tackle his friend. But Buzz stepped aside, snapping his red cape. Hamm skidded and kept sliding....

"Olé!" Trixie the Triceratops cried, clapping excitedly.

CRASH! Hamm slid right into the bookshelf. A single book teetered on the shelf and then fell right on top of Buzz. The room went silent. Was he … broken? For a moment, nothing moved. Suddenly, a hand reached around the cover of the book and Buzz pushed the book away.

"Buzz, are you okay?" Rex cried.

"Buzz, are you okay?" Buzz cried.

"Hey!" Rex turned to Hamm. "That's what I just said!"

Buzz blinked. "Hey! That's what I just said."

"No, that's what I said," Rex explained to Buzz.

"He must have gotten knocked into Repeat Mode!"
Hamm whispered to Buttercup the unicorn.

Buttercup trotted over to Buzz.

"Buttercup, you are the coolest unicorn in the universe," he said, grinning.

"Buttercup, you are the coolest unicorn in the universe," Buzz repeated.

The gang erupted into laughter.

"I'm not listening to this," Mr Potato Head said, yanking out his ears.

"What do we do?" Rex cried. Jessie had asked her friends to take care of Buzz. Now he was worse off than when she left!

"We're going to have to fix him before Bonnie and Jessie get home," Hamm said with a sigh. "Maybe we could try bouncing him on the bed to realign his wires."

The toys hauled Buzz onto the bed. "Jump!" Hamm said.

Rex jumped as high as he could and then landed. *BOING!*
Buzz flew right off the bed!

The rest of the toys climbed down to check on him. Buzz was lying
on the floor, motionless. The toys rolled him over. They tickled him.
They yelled at him. But it was no use.

Hamm glared at Rex. "Now what did you do?"

The toys heard a car pull into the driveway.

"They're home!" yelled Mr Pricklepants.

The peas hopped into their pod and hid.

"Hurry – we've got to fix Buzz!" Hamm shouted.

Rex undid Buzz's back panel and stared at all the wires.

"Which one?" Rex asked. "The red or the blue?"

Hamm looked at the wires and guessed. "Uh, blue, then red!"

"No! Red, then black!" cried Mr Potato Head. "Hurry!"

There was a noise outside the door. The toys went limp just as Bonnie's mother walked in and put down her daughter's backpack. The room was a mess!

"Bonnie!" Bonnie's mum started down the hall. "Please come clean up this room!"

"It is clean, Mum!" Bonnie called from the kitchen.

"Buzz, are you okay?" Jessie asked as she jumped out of Bonnie's backpack. Woody and Dolly were right behind her.

"Oh, uh, he's fine," Trixie said. She propped Buzz into a sitting position. Buzz fell over with a thunk.

"It's not my fault!" Rex wailed. "There are too many wires!"

Jessie shook her head and laughed. Then she whacked
Buzz on the back. Buzz blinked and looked at his friends.

"Do I have something on my face?" he asked.

The other toys sighed with relief. Buzz was back to normal!

"All right, all right, everyone!" Woody cried. "Now let's fix this
room before Bonnie comes back!" The toys went into action to tidy up.

Minutes later, Bonnie walked into her room. "Mum sure is picky," she said. Everything was perfectly tidy, just the way she had left it. Then she picked up Buzz. "Thanks for looking after everyone, Buzz. I knew this place would be okay with you in charge!"

FINDING NEMO

A Friend in Need

Nemo and his friends were about to go on their first expedition to Kelp Canyon. Marlin and Dory were their guides.

First, Dory went over the safety rules. "Rule number one: never leave your buddy behind," she said.

Everyone was listening closely – except for a green fish named Ward.

"I already know about safety. I could lead this trip myself," grumbled Ward.

After Dory finished the safety rules, the group set off. Before long, they came across Bruce the shark.

"G'day!" said Bruce.

"Aaaaaahhhhh!" screamed the fish. They had never seen a shark up close before!

But Nemo quickly piped up. "Don't worry. Bruce is my friend. We're not in any danger."

Just then, a plant caught Marlin's eye. "Now this plant is one you must avoid," Marlin instructed the group. "If you touch it, it will cause an itchy rash. Ohhh. Ahhh!" Marlin started scratching. He had accidentally touched the plant!

"I've got to get home," Marlin said. "Sorry, kids, we'll have to cancel the trip. You can't go without two leaders."

"I can be a leader!" Ward suggested. But the other fish just laughed at him.

Then Nemo had an idea. "What if Bruce is Dory's co-leader?"

Marlin thought for a moment. "Well, I suppose that would be all right. Just be careful!" he yelled as he headed home.

"I would love to help you, mates!" Bruce said. "I know a swell spot. It's better than Kelp Canyon. How would you like to explore a sunken pirate ship?"

"Yeah!" exclaimed almost all of the fish.

"What about you, mate?" Bruce asked Ward. "Doesn't that sound exciting?"

"We don't need you. I know lots of good spots," Ward replied jealously. "And I'm not your mate!"

I'll show this shark who should be co-leader! Ward thought.

Bruce led Dory and the young fish to the old sunken pirate ship.

"Here we are, mates!" Bruce said proudly. "Here's where I used to hang out when I was a mere nine-footer."

"Cool!" said Tad.

Nemo thought it looked a little scary and dangerous – but also very exciting. "I can't wait to go exploring!" he cried.

Inside the shipwreck, the group got separated. Nemo realized that Bruce and Ward had both disappeared. He sensed trouble.

Nemo found them on the deck of the ship.

"Bruce, I think I saw a fish stuck in that cage," Ward said.

"Really? Well, I've got to help him out – fish are friends!" Bruce said as he swam off to look inside the cage.

Nemo raced towards them. "Bruce! Look out! It's a trap!" he cried.

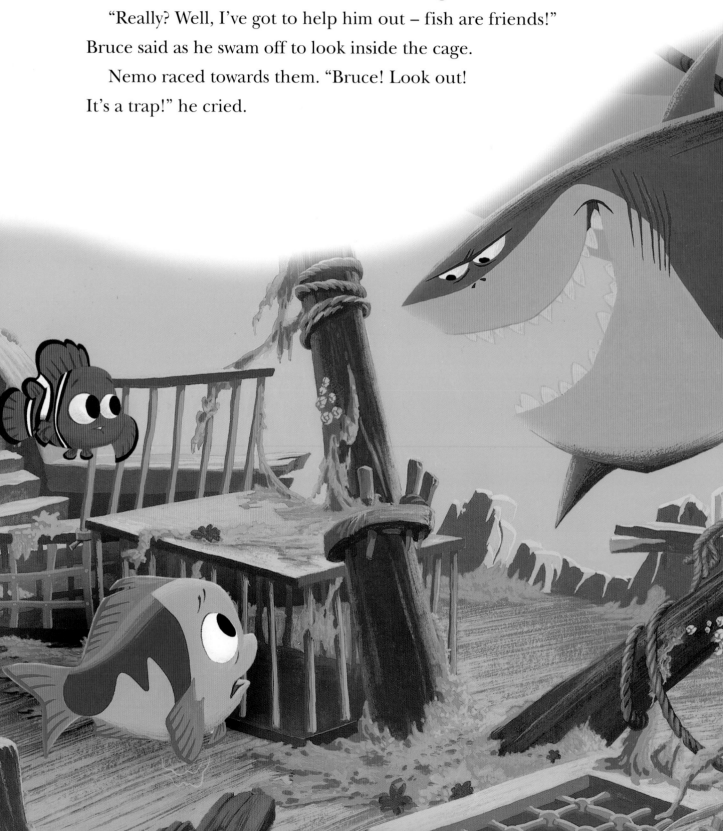

As soon as Bruce heard Nemo, he started bumping around inside the cage. Suddenly, the cage door closed with a *SLAM!*

"Ward!" shouted Nemo. "You just locked up my friend!"

"Good!" Ward shouted back. "Now I can be the co-leader." Ward sounded brave, but he raced away from the cage as fast as he could. After all, Bruce did have very large teeth!

"Don't worry, Bruce. I'll help you out," said Nemo, trying to open the cage. But it was no use. The door was stuck.

"I'll get Dory. Maybe she can help!" Nemo quickly swam off.

After searching through the ship, Nemo finally found Dory and the rest of the fish.

"I need help!" Nemo said urgently. "Ward locked Bruce up in a big cage."

"We don't need him anyway!" Ward said. "I can be the leader."

"You locked up Bruce?" Sheldon asked. "He's our buddy!"

"Yeah!" said the other fish. "Bruce is our friend!"

"Uh … I was just trying to …" began Ward. He suddenly felt nervous. He darted beneath a floorboard to hide.

But he got stuck! The fish tried to lift the board to pull Ward out, but they weren't strong enough. The board wouldn't budge.

"Just go home," said Ward with a grumble. "I don't need anyone's help anyway."

"No way," said Nemo. "Rule number one is: 'Never leave your buddy behind'."

"I'll bet Bruce could get him out of there," said Dory.

"But Bruce is stuck in a cage," Nemo reminded her.

"Oh," said Dory. "Well, we'll just have to get him out first!"

Dory instructed the other fish to stay put. Then she and Nemo raced off.

At the cage, Dory and Nemo pushed and pulled as hard as they could to get Bruce free. But the cage door wouldn't budge.

"Bruce, you've got to break free. Ward got stuck and he needs your help," Nemo said.

That was all Bruce needed to hear.

CRRRAAACKKK! He broke right through the cage!

Then he swam over to Ward, and with his mighty strength, Bruce freed him!

"Hooray!" shouted the other fish.

On the way home, Ward apologized to Bruce.
"I'm sorry," he said. "I guess I have a lot to learn.
I thought I was ready to be a co-leader."

"No worries," Bruce said kindly. "I shouldn't have taken you to such a dangerous place. It looks like we both have a lot to learn. So, are we mates?"

Ward was thrilled and relieved that Bruce wasn't mad at him. "Mates!" he said excitedly. After all, he had never had a shark for a friend before!

A little later, Nemo swam over to Bruce. "Thanks for saving Ward, even though he wasn't being nice," Nemo said.

"Aw, it was nothing, mate," replied Bruce. "Besides, that's what friends are for!"

Rematch!

Lightning McQueen and Francesco Bernoulli had challenged each other to a race in Monza, Italy – Francesco's hometown.

"Benvenuto!" said Francesco. "Your plane was late, but this is no surprise. You will be late crossing the finish line, too."

Lightning smiled. Then he whispered to Mater, "I am so beating him – right here on his own turf!"

As they left the airport, the cars were surrounded by photographers.

"Paparazzi love Francesco. He has too many fans," said Francesco.

"Nobody has more fans than Lightning!" Mater piped up.

Francesco rolled his eyes.

"We will prove it!" said Luigi. "Lightning gets hundreds of fan letters each day. Guido, bring the mailbags!"

Guido zoomed off!

Guido returned with a mailbag overflowing with fan letters.

Lightning was a little embarrassed. "Oh, it's really not that big a deal," he said.

"You are right, Lightning," said Francesco. "It is no big deal because Francesco has much, much more fan mail!"

"Letters are great," said Lightning. "But we like to get some fender-to-fender time with our fans whenever we can."

Lightning and his friends greeted all the cars that were lined up to see them.

Mater revved up the crowd. They began chanting: "Light-NING! Light-NING!"

"Questo é ridicolo!" grumbled Francesco. "And what about autographs?" he asked. "Watch – and be amazed!"

Francesco started spinning his wheels and spewing out hundreds of autographed photos of himself to his fans. "See? Francesco always gets things done at 300 kilometres an hour."

After the two racers had greeted their fans, they drove to a café.

"Hey, Mr Francesco, nobody drinks oil faster than Lightning,"
Mater said.

"What?" Lightning cried. "Mater, I can't drink –"

"C'mon buddy, show 'em what I done taught you!" Mater exclaimed.

Lightning sighed and managed to finish a can of oil in a few gulps.

Francesco was not impressed. "Francesco never guzzles," he said. "Oil should be savoured."

Lightning turned to Francesco. "How about a warm-up before the big race – just you and me?" he asked.

Francesco nodded. "Ah, good idea, Lightning! Try to keep up, if you…."

But before Francesco could finish, Lightning had become a red streak down the road!

"Ka-ciao, Francesco!" Lightning yelled.

Francesco was just about to catch up with Lightning when he nearly spun out on a left turn.

"How do you make those left turns so smoothly?" Francesco asked Lightning.

"Get equipped with some treaded tyres," Lightning explained. "Then turn right to go left. A very good friend taught me that once."

The race cars finally stopped to rest.

Francesco sighed. "Ah, Italy is beautiful, no? Just like Francesco!"

Lightning chuckled. "Do you always think about yourself?" he asked.

"Of course," Francesco replied. "On the racetrack, Francesco only thinks about himself and doing his best. This is why he always wins!"

The next day was the big race. Finally, the world
would find out who was the fastest race car.

When the flag dropped, the fans went wild!

After the first left turn, Francesco came out ahead. He showed off his
new treaded tyres. "Perhaps Lightning has taught Francesco too well!"

Lightning couldn't help but smile.

The racers each entered the Monza arena and made a pit stop.

As Lightning zoomed out of the pits, he heard his friends and fans cheering for him. Then the flashing of some cameras distracted him.

Suddenly, Lightning remembered what Francesco had said about focusing on himself and doing his best. Lightning looked straight ahead – and took the lead!

CAR BONARA

As the two cars crossed the finish line,
the crowd gasped.

"Ka-chow!" yelled Lightning. "I won!"

"You mean ciao bella!" cried Francesco.
"Francesco won!"

The race cars and the fans looked to the judges.
The crowd gasped again. The race was a … TIE!

Back in the pit garage, the cars tried to figure out what to do about the tie.

Suddenly, Francesco shouted, "No more talk! Talk is slow. What do we do? We race!"

"Right," Lightning agreed. "We'll race again in Radiator Springs!"

"That's a great idea!" Mater said excitedly. "We can have a tractor-tipping contest!"

Francesco rolled his eyes. "Tractor tipping is boring. You know the Leaning Tower of Tyres? Francesco put the 'Leaning' in it. Francesco can tip anything."

Lightning laughed. "C'mon! Last one to
Radiator Springs has to guzzle down oil!"
The two fastest cars in the world zoomed
away together ... to race again another day.